T0090695

Joseph and the Colorful Coat

Copyright © 2015 by Brendan Powell Smith

LEGO® is a trademark of the LEGO Group of companies which does not sponsor, authorize or endorse this book.

All rights reserved. No part of this book may be reproduced in any manner without the express written consent of the publisher, except in the case of brief excerpts in critical reviews or articles. All inquiries should be addressed to Sky Pony Press, 307 West 36th Street, 11th Floor, New York, NY 10018.

Sky Pony Press books may be purchased in bulk at special discounts for sales promotion, corporate gifts, fund-raising, or educational purposes. Special editions can also be created to specifications. For details, contact the Special Sales Department, Sky Pony Press, 307 West 36th Street, 11th Floor, New York, NY 10018 or info@skyhorsepublishing.com.

Sky Pony® is a registered trademark of Skyhorse Publishing, Inc®, a Delaware corporation.

Visit our website at www.skyponypress.com.

10 9 8 7 6 5 4 3 2 1

Manufactured in China, December 2014
This product conforms to CPSIA 2008

Library of Congress Cataloging-in-Publication Data

Smith, Brendan Powell, author.
Joseph and the colorful coat : the Brick Bible for kids / Brendan Powell Smith.
    pages cm.—(The Brick Bible for kids)
Summary: "The story of Jacob and his sons, the colorful coat, and Joseph in Egypt is a timeless tale about love, jealousy, and, ultimately, forgiveness. Now, for the first time, this incredible story comes to life as part of The Brick Bible for Kids series"—Provided by publisher.
Audience: Ages 3-5.
Audience: Pre-school.
ISBN 978-1-63220-409-7 (hc : alk. paper)
1. Joseph (Son of Jacob)—Juvenile literature. 2. Brothers—Juvenile literature. 3. Jealousy—Juvenile literature. 4. Bible stories, English—Genesis. I. Title.
BS580.J6S47 2015
222.1109505—dc23
                         2014034581

Cover design by Brian Peterson
Cover photograph credit Brendan Powell Smith

Ebook ISBN: 978-1-63220-828-6

Editor: Julie Matysik
Designer: Brian Peterson
Production Manager: Sara Kitchen

Joseph and the Colorful Coat

THE BRICK BIBLE for Kids

Brendan Powell Smith

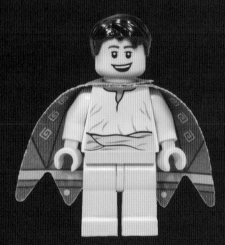

Sky Pony Press
New York

Jacob was an old shepherd with twelve sons. The youngest sons were Joseph and Benjamin. Jacob loved Joseph more than all of his other sons. When Joseph was seventeen years old, his father gave him a special gift—a very colorful coat.

Joseph had strange dreams and told his brothers about them. In his dreams Joseph saw all his brothers bowing down before him. When they heard this, his older brothers got angry and said, "So, you think you are better than us? You think you will rule over us?" Joseph's older brothers hated him.

One day, Jacob sent Joseph to check on his older brothers who were watching the family's goats and sheep in the countryside. "Here comes the little dreamer," said his brothers when they saw Joseph approaching, and they quickly made a plan to get rid of him for good.

As soon as Joseph arrived, his brothers grabbed him, tore off his colorful coat, and tossed him into a well that was so deep he couldn't climb out. "Let's see what becomes of his dreams now!" they said.

Shortly afterward, the brothers saw some traveling merchants approaching, and they said, "Let's not leave our brother to die. Let's sell him instead." So they pulled Joseph up out of the well and sold him as a slave to the traveling merchants.

On their way back home, the brothers took Joseph's colorful coat and smeared it with blood from a goat. When they showed it to Jacob, he was deeply heartbroken and said, "My poor son, Joseph! A wild animal must have eaten him!"

Meanwhile, the traveling merchants took Joseph all the way to the land of Egypt. There they sold him to a rich Egyptian man named Potiphar, and Joseph became one of his household slaves.

During his years as a slave, Joseph was successful
at every task he performed. Potiphar noticed that
Joseph must be blessed by God, so he promoted
him to be his personal assistant. Eventually, he put
Joseph in charge of his entire household.

Potiphar's wife had noticed that Joseph was very handsome. She would often try to kiss Joseph, but Joseph always turned away. This made her very angry, and one day when Joseph refused to kiss her, she screamed so loud that her husband came running.

When Potiphar arrived, his wife lied to him about Joseph, saying that Joseph had tried to kiss her. Potiphar believed his wife, and he became so angry at Joseph that he had Joseph arrested and thrown in prison.

God still watched over Joseph in prison. When Joseph's fellow prisoners had strange dreams, they would tell him their dreams, and with God's help Joseph always explained exactly what the dream revealed about the future, and he was always right.

One night, Pharaoh, the king of Egypt, had a troubling dream. He very badly wanted to know its meaning, so the next day he gathered all the magicians and wise men in Egypt to his palace and he described his troubling dream to them.

But none of the magicians and wise men could understand Pharaoh's dream or tell him what it meant. Then one of Pharaoh's servants spoke up and said: "I once met a man in prison named Joseph who can explain the meaning of any dream."

So Pharaoh had Joseph taken out of prison and brought before him. "I am told you have the power to explain the meaning of any dream," Pharaoh said. "It is not my power, but God's," replied Joseph. "Tell me your dream."

Pharaoh told Joseph that in his dream there were seven fat, healthy cows that came up out of the Nile River. They were then followed by seven scrawny, sickly cows. The skinny cows ate up the fat cows. And that's when Pharaoh

"This is what your dream means," said Joseph. "Egypt will have seven good years of plentiful food followed by seven years of terrible famine when no food will grow. If Pharaoh is wise, he will put someone in charge who will store the extra food from the plentiful years so there is still food to eat during the years of famine."

"Since God has given you such wisdom, there can be no one better suited for the job than you," said Pharaoh to Joseph. "You shall serve as governor over all my lands. I put my entire kingdom in your power, and my people shall obey your commands."

As Joseph predicted, Egypt then had seven years
of plenty during which more grain was grown
than all the Egyptians could eat. As governor,
Joseph made sure all the extra food was safely
locked away in Pharaoh's great storehouses.

Then the years of terrible famine arrived, and no food was able to grow anywhere. The only food around was in Egypt thanks to Joseph's careful planning. Starving people from all the surrounding lands traveled to Egypt to buy food from Joseph.

In Joseph's homeland of Israel, the famine was severe, and the elderly Jacob said to his eleven remaining sons, "Why are you all just standing around here while we starve? Travel to Egypt where they have food and bring some back home!"

So the brothers set out, and when they reached
Egypt, they bowed down before the governor and
humbly asked for food. They did not recognize that
the governor was their own brother Joseph. But
Joseph recognized his brothers.

Joseph wondered if his brothers had changed their ways
after all these years, so he decided to test them. He had
their sacks filled with grain, but he also hid some money
in their sacks. And in his younger brother Benjamin's
sack, he hid his own silver drinking cup.

Joseph sent them on their way home, but soon afterward
he chased them down as they were leaving the city.
"Why have you stolen from me after I was kind and gave
you food?" shouted Joseph. He had their sacks opened

The brothers were shocked and confused. They said to themselves that God must now be punishing them for the awful thing they did to their brother so many years ago. "Because your youngest brother stole my cup," said Joseph. "I will keep him as my slave."

At this the oldest brother begged Joseph to take him as a slave instead of Benjamin. He told Joseph that their father had already lost one of his sons, and to now lose the youngest son would break his heart forever.

Joseph now saw that his brothers had indeed changed their ways and he could pretend no longer. "Look closely! Don't you recognize me? I am your brother Joseph," he told them. "Now, go return to our father and bring him and all of our family here to Egypt."

Jacob was amazed and overjoyed to learn that his
son Joseph was still alive. He took his entire family
and traveled down to Egypt. When they finally
met again after so many years, Joseph and Jacob

Pharaoh was grateful to Joseph and he gave Joseph's
family the best land in Egypt for their new home.
Joseph was not angry with his brothers for what they
did to him when he was young, because he knew it

Activity!

Can you find these ten brick pieces in the book?
On which page does each appear?
The answers are below.

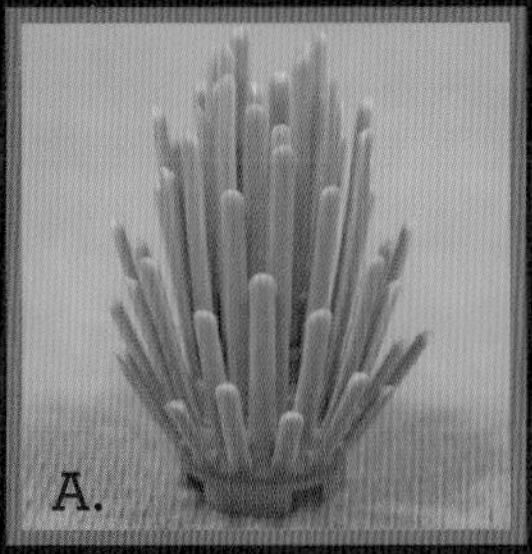
A.

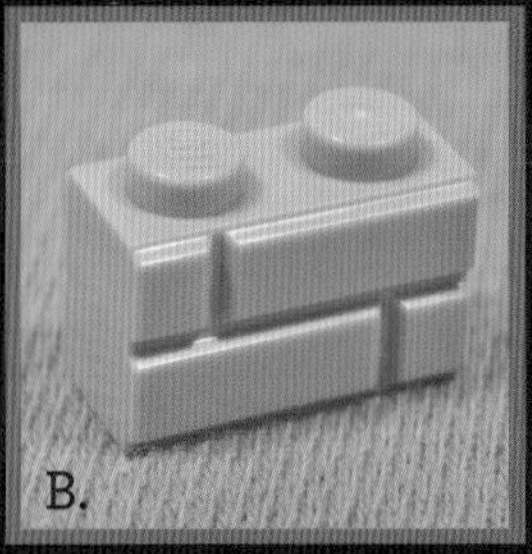
B.

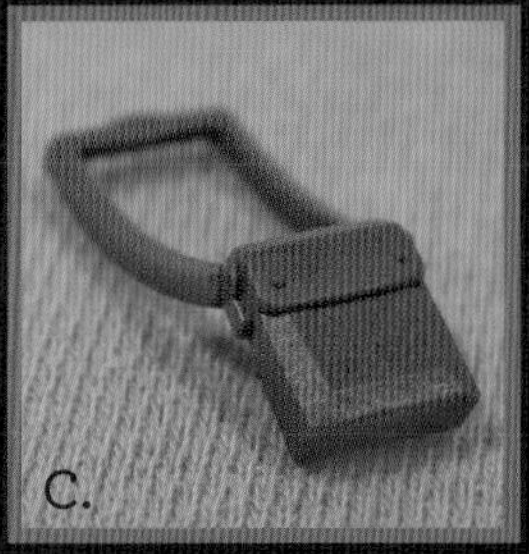
C.

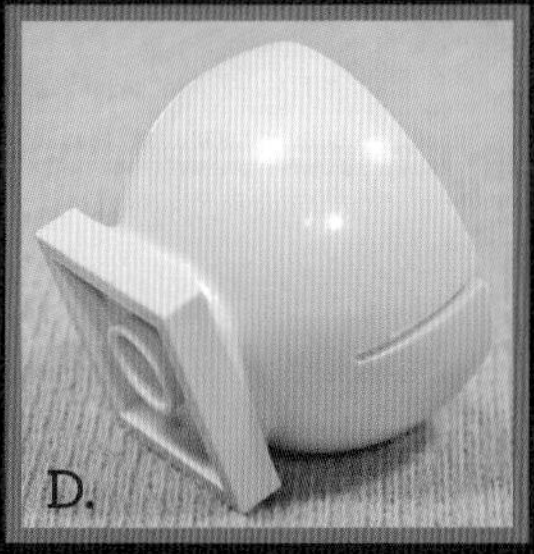
D.

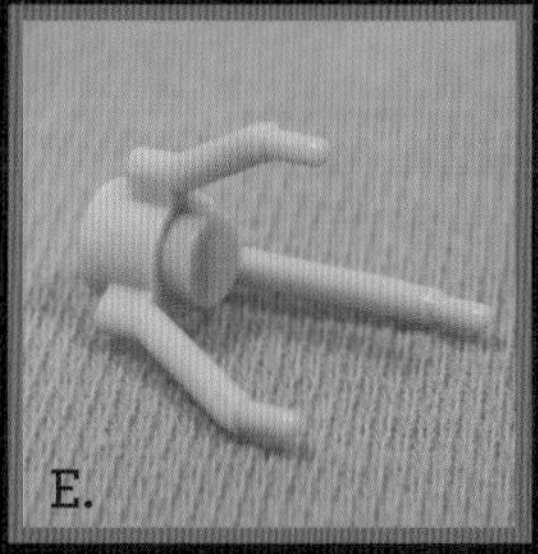
E.

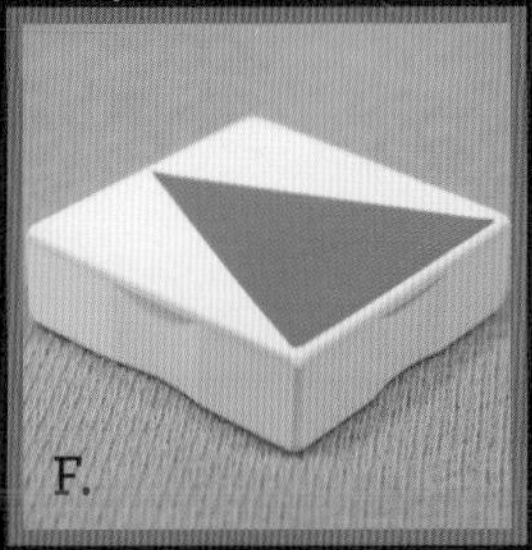
F.

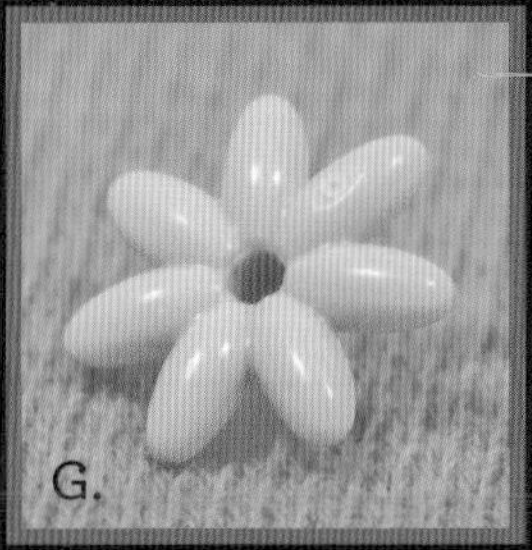
G.

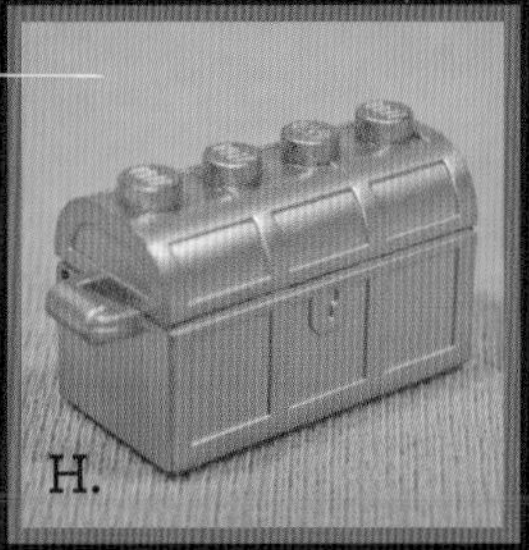
H.

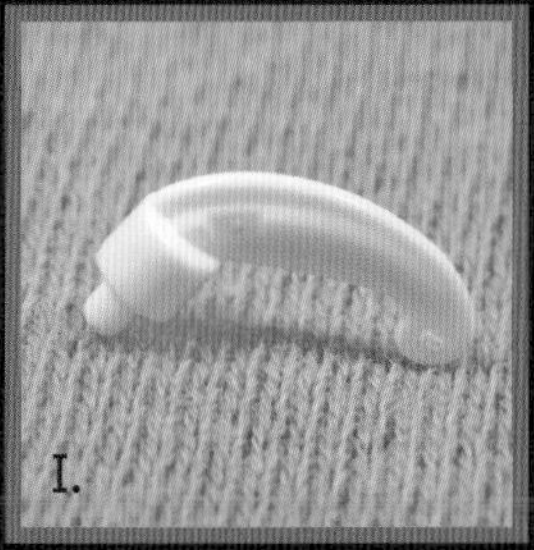
I.

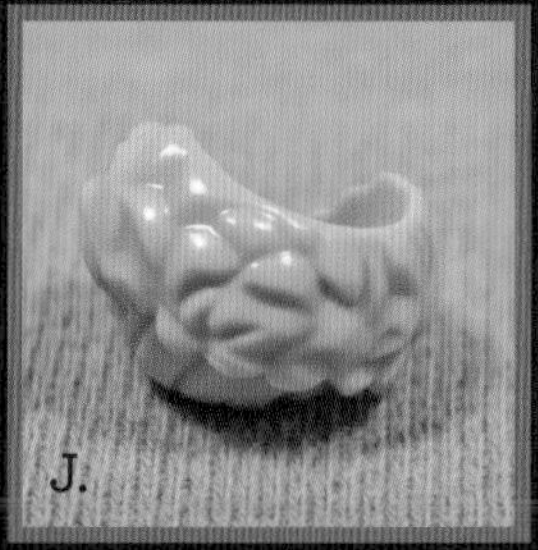
J.

Answer key:

A: p. 23, B: p. 7, C: p. 8, D: p. 13, E: p. 21, F: p. 15, G: p. 31, H: p. 30, I: p. 11, J: p. 16